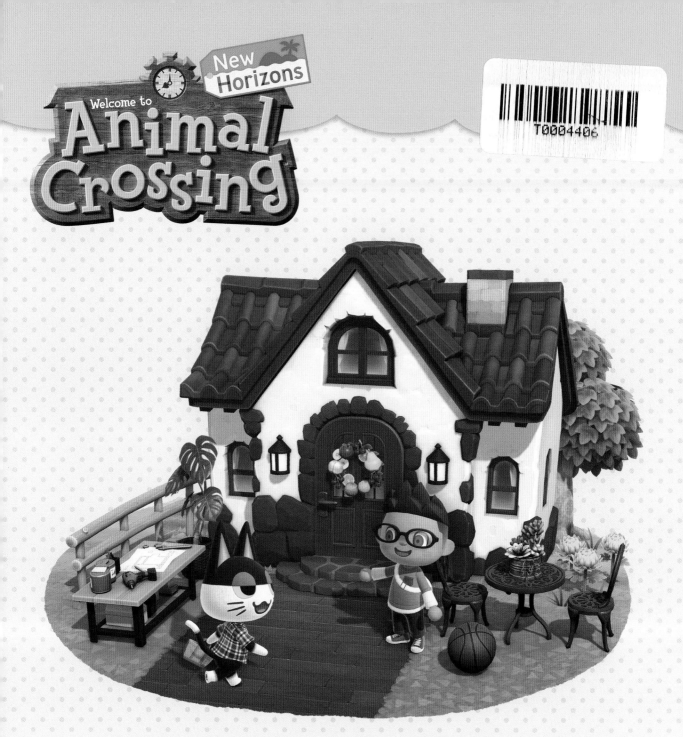

Official Activity Book

By Steve Foxe

Designed by Melanie Bermudez Cerna

Random House 🏠 New York

ISBN 978-0-593-37364-4 (trade)
rhcbooks.com
MANUFACTURED IN CHINA
10 9 8 7 6 5 4 3

Welcome to your very own island paradise! Design a home, invite animal residents to become your neighbors, dig for fossils, collect bugs, go fishing, craft new items, and visit other islands to make new friends. Relax and have fun with **Animal Crossing: New Horizons!**

How many words can you make out of **Animal Crossing**?
Try to come up with ten!

1. _____

2. _____

3. _____

4. _____

5. _____

6. _____

7. _____

8. _____

9. _____

10. _____

How about **New Horizons**? Try to think of 15 this time!

1. _____

2. _____

3. _____

4. _____

5. _____

6. _____

7. _____

8. _____

9. _____

10. _____

11. _____

12. _____

13. _____

14. _____

15. _____

See all answers on pages 31 and 32.

Can you draw yourself in the style of Animal Crossing: New Horizons?
Draw yourself as one of the neighbors.

Isabelle keeps the residents up to date on special events and rates your island's progress. She can even help you design your island's flag!

Draw your idea for an island flag.

Nook Inc.!

Tom Nook owns Nook Inc., and Resident Services. He helps build homes and will help you develop your island. Use your stickers to complete the scene!

6

Nook Shopping

Timmy and Tommy are Tom Nook's protégés. They run Nook's Cranny, a shop Tom Nook used to manage. Unscramble the words to discover some of the items you can buy in their shop.

1. HELOVS   — — — — — —

2. LALUERBM   — — — — — — — —

3. HOGSLSNIT   — — — — — — — — —

4. TRGNAEWI NAC   — — — — — — — —   — — —

5. HGINSIF ORD   — — — — — — —   — — —

Wilbur and Orville run Dodo Airlines.
These coworkers can fly you to other islands to meet
potential new neighbors and visit your friends.
Help them find their way back to the airport!

The smooth sounds of your island are provided by the one and only K.K. Slider. Draw yourself playing your favorite instrument.

Flick is a bug enthusiast. He visits your island to host the Bug-Off and hands out rewards! Can you find the names of these insects and arachnids? Look forward, backward, up, and down. Use your stickers to add even more bugs to the page!

BUTTERFLY • GOLIATH • BEETLE • CENTIPEDE
MOSQUITO • CRICKET • FLEA • TARANTULA
MOTH • FIREFLY • ANT WASP • CICADA
DRAGONFLY • SNAIL • SCORPION • LADYBUG

M	D	R	A	G	O	N	F	L	Y	U	W	A	S	P
M	G	B	L	G	U	B	Y	D	A	L	T	S	G	P
O	M	Y	W	A	D	E	G	U	F	M	O	C	O	Y
S	O	B	U	T	T	E	R	F	L	Y	F	O	L	L
Q	T	S	E	G	H	T	O	P	E	R	E	R	I	F
U	H	O	T	R	A	L	S	N	A	I	L	P	A	E
I	C	R	I	C	K	E	T	A	F	D	S	I	T	R
T	J	C	I	C	A	D	A	M	N	B	C	O	H	I
O	I	T	E	D	E	P	I	T	N	E	C	N	R	F
E	A	N	T	A	A	L	U	T	N	A	R	A	T	G

Instead of bugs, C.J. has an eye for fish. Use the code to unscramble the names of some of these underwater creatures. Use your stickers to give C.J. even more fish to admire!

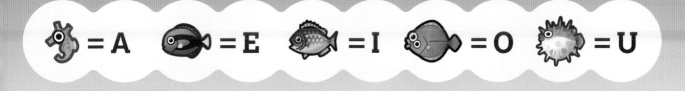

= A   = E   = I   = O   = U

H_MM_RH__D SH_RK

ST_RF_SH

M_H_-M_H_

R_BB_N __L

__RF_SH

SN_PP_NG T_RTL_

Can you spot all five differences between these two summer scenes?

Hide-and-Seek!

The neighbors on the island love to play games. See if you can find all their hiding spots!

Start at the arrow, and, going clockwise, write every third letter in order on the blanks to see what Blathers finds in the museum.

_ _ _ _ _ _ _ _

F S D O W K S Y X S B G I D J L P M S E A

Celeste is Blathers's sister. She knows all about stars and constellations. Look at the patterns. Figure out what the next two star fragments in each row should be, and use your stickers to fill them in.

GET CRAFTING!

When you live on an island, you have to get crafty!
Use your stickers to decorate.

A special tool can help you cross rivers and other bodies of water. To find out what the tool is called, replace each letter below with the one that comes after it in the alphabet and write them on the blanks.

N G U T L A I V   E P L O

_ _ _ _ _ _ _ _   _ _ _ _

Able Sisters is the island's premier clothing store. To learn the names of the sisters, cross out the letters of the alphabet that are in order. Write the remaining letters on the blanks.

ABSCDEAFGBHILJEKLMMNOABPQRESLTULAVWXBYEZL

__ __ __ __ __, __ __ __ __ __, __ __ __ __ __

Island life is always full of activity. Study the scene for three minutes. Then cover the picture to see how well you can remember all the colorful details.

Now let's test your memory.

1. Which tool is the character on the bottom left holding?

   _____

2. What color is the roof in the background?

   _____

3. Not counting the players, how many neighbors are in the picture? _____

4. What is the neighbor in the lower right corner doing?

   _____

5. Is there a bridge in the picture?

   _____

A Day in the Life!
Use your stickers to complete the scene.

K	K	I	C	K	S	S	C	S	K	I	S	K	S	C
C	S	C	K	I	C	S	K	I	C	K	S	K	S	C
K	C	K	I	C	I	C	S	C	K	I	C	I	C	K
I	C	K	C	K	S	K	K	I	C	K	S	C	K	I
C	K	K	I	S	K	S	K	I	K	I	C	K	S	C
K	I	C	K	I	C	K	S	C	S	K	I	S	C	K
S	C	K	S	C	S	K	I	C	K	S	S	K	S
C	K	S	K	I	S	C	K	C	K	C	K	I	C	S
C	S	K	S	K	I	C	K	S	I	K	S	C	K	I
S	K	C	K	I	S	K	I	C	I	K	I	C	K	S

How many times can
you find the word

KICKS

in the puzzle?

Tropical Paradise!

23

Fruit Frenzy!

Every island has its own native fruit tree.
Use your stickers to match the patterns in the first box.

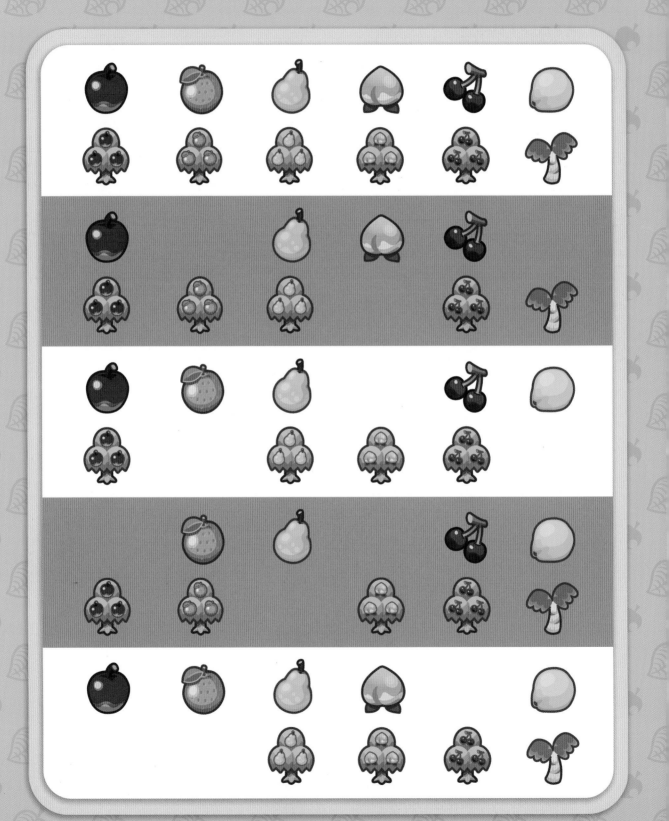

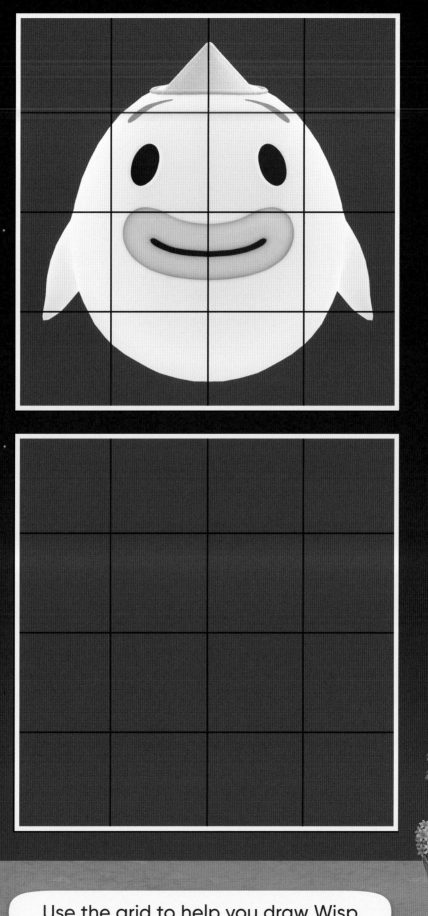

Use the grid to help you draw Wisp.

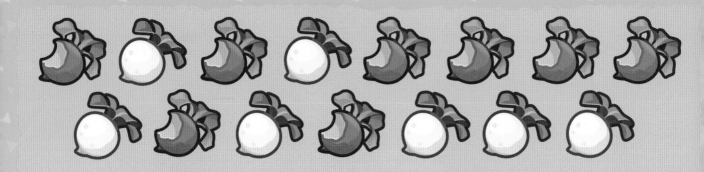

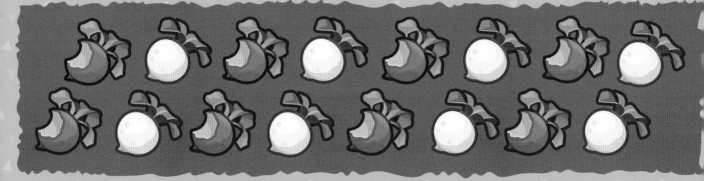

Daisy Mae is new to the turnip-selling business, and she just dropped her latest batch everywhere! Can you help her count the spilled turnips? Don't count the rotten ones!

Harvey runs his own photo studio, called Photopia.
Use your character stickers to make your own memories here.

Raymond wants to move to your island!
Help him find his way to the campsite.

START

FINISH

Something is always happening in the world of
Animal Crossing: New Horizons.
Use your stickers to make this island your own!

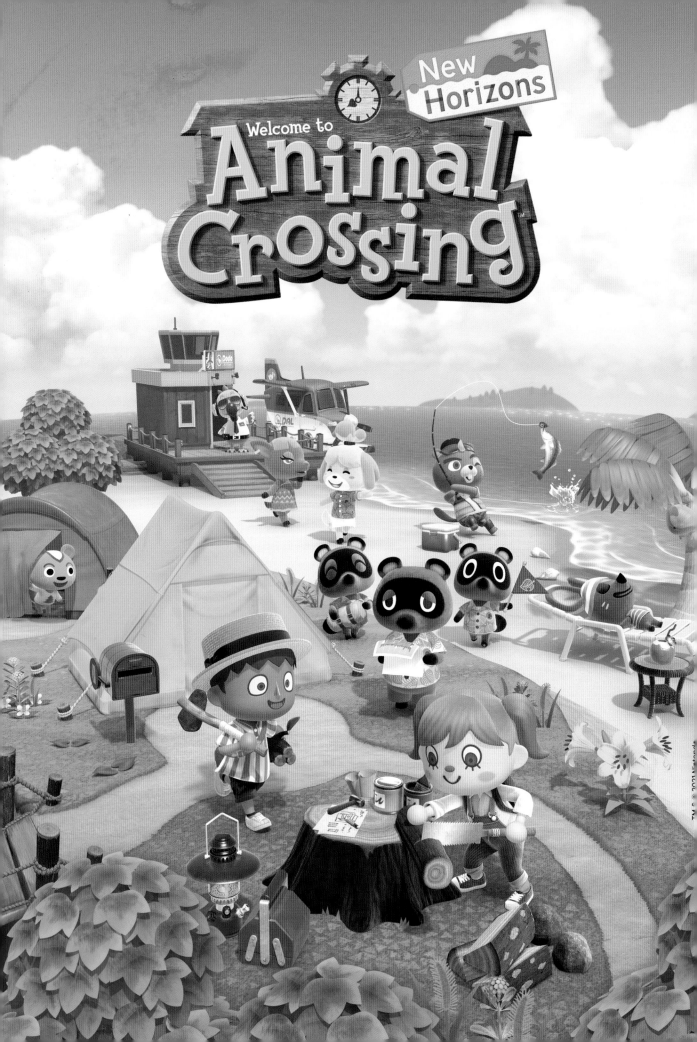

Answers

Page 3

Possible answers for Animal Crossing:
Acorns, again, arm, canal, coils, coral, mail, mango, micro, minor, moss, ocarina, sailor, silo, smiling, snail, solar, and songs.

Possible answers for New Horizons:
Her, heron, honor, horn, newish, news, nine, noise, none, noon, nose, one, onion, onshore, oozes, own, owner, ozone, rhinos, rinse, rise, senior, sew, siren, snore, son, sooner, winners, wire, worsen, and zones.

Page 6

Page 7

1. shovel
2. umbrella
3. slingshot
4. watering can
5. fishing rod

Page 8

Page 10

Page 11

hammerhead shark
starfish
mahi-mahi
ribbon eel
oarfish
snapping turtle

Page 12

In the bottom picture, the player's eyes are brown, the watering can is blue, the butterfly is missing, the door wreath is missing, and there are apples on the tree.

Page 13

Answers

Page 14

fossils

Page 15

Page 17

vaulting pole

Page 18

Sable, Mabel, Label

Page 19

1. shovel
2. red
3. five
4. watering the flowers
5. yes

Page 22

```
K K I C K K S S C S K I S K S C
C S C K I C S K I C K S K K S C
K C K I C I C S C K I C I C K
I C K C K S K K I C K S C K I
C K K I S K S K I K I C K S C
K I C K I C K S C S K I S C K
S C K S C S K K I C K S S K S
C K S K I S C K C K C K I C S
C S K S K I C K S I K S C K I
S K C K I S K I C K I C K S
```

Page 23

In the bottom picture, the 6 on Jay's T-shirt is an 8, the player's tank top is purple, the butterfly Flick is catching is missing, the beach ball is missing, and O'Hare's shirt is pink.

Page 24

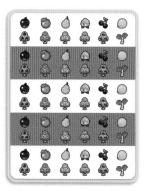

Page 26

28 turnips

Page 28